CW01506827

MERRY CHRISTMAS, MISS PENNY

A SWEETLY SPOOKY CHRISTMAS ROMANCE SHORT STORY

MISHA CREWS

FREE BOOK

To read my full-length Christmas novel *The Book of Forgotten Angels,* go to MishaCrews.com/freebook, or click this link in your ebook.

I

"Hey, mister," a tiny voice called up through the cold winter air. "What're you doing way up there?"

Ryan leaned over so he could look down, and his heart skipped a beat. Three pairs of eyes — wide, innocent, and full of wonder — stared up at him. Two of the pairs were an identical shade of blue and belonged to a couple of apple-cheeked blond children wearing matching blue coats. The third pair of eyes was as black as coal and set in a pale, somber little face.

Ryan was hanging about eighty feet above the ground with his legs dangling from a harness as he worked. His assistant, Edgar, was tied off a few feet to his right, clipping cable onto the tower. At the sight of the children, the two men looked at each other, and one word flashed between them: *danger*.

Ryan leaned back over. "Scram!" he yelled. "Get out of here! It's not safe!" This was a work area, for God's sake: hardhats only. If he or Edgar dropped a wrench or pair of clippers…. He looked around and saw the third member of the crew over by the truck. "Hey Auggie, get these kids out of here! What are you thinking, man?"

But Auggie, who'd been alerted by the first syllable of "Hey, mister," was already moving. Auggie herded the little urchins away from the monopine, limping a little on his false leg, a souvenir from the Middle East. The kids squawked like angry pigeons, but they went along.

Ryan allowed himself a small smile as he watched them go. They were actually kind of cute. He thought the blond children, a boy and a girl, were twins and probably a handful. The third one, with the dark hair and eyes, was quiet and a little sullen-looking, but obviously curious. Ryan wondered where their mother was and whether she was worried.

Ryan spoke a few words to Edgar and put his attention back on the tower and the work at hand. Knowing Auggie, he would give the kids some candy and send them on their way. Auggie had a tender heart for children. Ryan wasn't quite as soft and cuddly, but he couldn't afford to be. He was the boss, at least on this site. It was his responsibility to make sure the job got done. Neither of his guys wanted to be out here fixing cellular antennas two days before Christmas, but work was work. Ryan had never really cared much about holidays, so it was nothing to him.

He was just getting focused again when a woman's voice could be heard calling through the trees. "Jennifer! Jacob! Where are you? Are you out here?" The woman sounded nearly frantic. This had to be the mom.

"Oh, brother," Ryan muttered. He and Edgar glanced at each other again. "Trouble." Most moms would flip out if they caught their kids in the woods with a bunch of strange men.

Ryan disconnected the positioning lanyard, clipped it onto his belt, squeezed the descender on his harness, and started zipping downward. He was still a dozen feet from the ground when a woman came marching through the trees. Her posture was graceful and full of purpose. She had dark hair which was tied back in a ponytail, and she wore an oversized orange parka with a fur-rimmed hood that bounced on her back as she moved. Even from this height he could make out her elfin nose and the slender fingers peeking from the ends of her coat sleeves. She was a very pretty lady, and she was wearing a very angry expression.

Ryan's feet touched ground just as she caught sight of the children. Her face melted with relief. "There you are! What are you doing back here?

Haven't I told you not to play in these woods? Honestly…"

Then her tired brown eyes landed on Auggie and the truck. She stopped short, her expression alarmed and watchful. She lowered her voice. "Kids, come here, right now."

The kids moved to her side without a single word of protest. When they were within arm's reach, she looped her arms around their shoulders and lifted her chin. She spoke sternly. "Who are you? And what are you doing here? This is private property."

"Yes, ma'am," Auggie said humbly. He was well over six foot four, and with his long hair and full beard, he looked mighty intimidating. He was the actually sweetest guy ever, but of course this woman couldn't be expected to know that. "We're with Eastern Tower and Steel. We're just doing some work on the tower here."

"What tower? What are you talking about?" The authority in her voice was forced, anyone could hear that.

"This one," Ryan said.

She jumped and her head snapped in his direction. She glared him a good one.

Well, shoot. He hadn't meant to startle her. He gestured back over his shoulder. "See that pine tree? It's actually a cellular tower. What we call a stealth tower."

The woman and the three children all turned their heads to look at it. Ryan didn't bother turning around. He knew what they were seeing: a 110-foot cellular tower with fake branches coming out on all sides of it. Up close, it looked like a giant streetlight pole with pipe cleaners stuck in it. But from far away, you wouldn't even know it was there. It just blended in with the tree line.

"Cool," the kids intoned in unison.

Ryan smiled. His thoughts, exactly. "We're doing some work on one of the antennas. We'll be done today—tomorrow, latest."

Mom didn't look happy or impressed by that. "And do you have permission to be here? I know the owner of this land, and I can check, so don't bother lying to me."

"Oh yes, ma'am. Eastern Tower does things by the book. I admit I've never talked to the owner myself. We're too far down on the food chain for something like that, but you can be sure that the proper permissions were obtained before we were sent out here." He fished a business card out of his pocket and took a few steps in her direction, holding it out to her.

She looked at it doubtfully. Ryan felt like a wildlife photographer trying to coax a timid deer into the light so he could get a good picture. He held his position, with his arm extended, and finally, the woman reached out and took the card.

Examining it, she seemed slightly mollified. "All right then. Don't stay any longer than you have to." She watched as Auggie tossed a candy wrapper onto the ground. "And don't litter," she snapped. "What, do you expect the squirrels to pick up after you?"

"Sorry, ma'am," Auggie said meekly, stooping to pick it up.

She gave them all a warning look, turned herself and the kids around, and marched away.

The men looked at each other and laughed.

"I think that's the signal that it's time for lunch," Ryan said.

2

The crew's good mood didn't last long. They were definitely going to need to spend another day on this site. Ryan knew his bosses weren't going to be any happier than his crew was, but what choice did they have? The job had to get done.

On the way back to the motel, he saw the twins outside a small, neat house. They were shooting a basketball at a hoop that had been improvised out of an old clothes hanger nailed to a tree. The dark-haired child was there as well, but he was playing on his own, separate from the other two. On impulse, Ryan applied the brake and rolled down the window. "Hey, kids," he called.

The twins turned toward him simultaneously, startling him with their doll-like synchronicity. "Hi, mister!"

They got up and ran toward him, but stopped at the curb, well out of arm's reach. Ryan smiled. Seemed like a couple somebodies had gotten a recent lecture on stranger danger. Good thing, that. Parents couldn't be too careful these days.

The dark-haired boy stayed where he was, but his eyes were murky beacons that sought Ryan's face. Poor kid, all on his own like that. When Ryan spoke, he directed his words to the dark-eyed boy as well as the twins.

"Tell your mom that we're going to be back tomorrow to finish up, so she shouldn't worry if she sees us," Ryan said.

"Can we come up and watch you work?"

Ryan laughed. "Um, I don't think your mother would like that very much."

"She's not our mother," they said. "She's Miss Penny."

Huh. Must've been the babysitter, after all. She sure had acted like a mother: overprotective, bossy, and loving all at the same time. Guess she took her job seriously. "Okay, well tell Miss Penny that she's likely to see us around here again, okay? I don't want her to be concerned."

"Okay."

The four blue eyes roamed hungrily over the truck, and Ryan could tell they were dying to see what was inside. He'd been just like that when he was their age. But that was a long time ago.

. . .

RYAN HALF EXPECTED to see the kids sneaking around the job site the following day. But to his surprise, it was Miss Penny herself who showed up, still as bold as brass, but looking somewhat friendlier.

The boys had just broken for lunch, and they were huddled inside the truck, where it was warm. She knocked on the window, and Ryan jumped. When he saw who it was, he got out of the truck and closed the door behind him.

He started to speak, "Now, miss, we're almost finished, and we'll be out of your hair soon enough. So please—"

She waved her hand. "I came to apologize. I was rude yesterday, but it was just because I was worried about the children. They may look innocent as angels, but they're far from it. They like to run off sometimes. They're not mean, but they're just…"

She trailed off and Ryan finished for her. "Kids."

She smiled, and Ryan's heart did a little dance. "Right. Well, I called Mr. Everett, who owns this land, and he says you're okay to be here. So, I'm sorry for being rude yesterday."

"Don't worry about it."

"Well, no worries on this end."

"Thank you." She stood there, looking uncomfortable.

Ryan wasn't sure what he was supposed to say.

Then she spoke again. "There's something else. The children are really fascinated by your truck and the work you do. I was wondering if it would be possible for you and your men to come by when you're finished here and show them your tools. I like to encourage them to think about the kind of work they might want to do when they get older."

Ryan didn't know what to say. "You're a hell of a babysitter," he blurted. "Those kids are damn lucky."

She flushed. "I'm not their babysitter. I'm their foster mother."

"So that's why…"

"That's why they call me 'Miss Penny,'" she finished for him. "I run a foster home. I always have children in my house."

"Wow." Ryan didn't know what to say to that, either. Penny was a young woman. She seemed smart, and she was certainly good-looking. There were probably a lot of things she could be doing with her life besides taking care of a bunch of kids.

She spoke again. "So you'll come this evening, or whenever you're finished?"

"Of course."

She held out a hand. "By the way, my name is Penelope Daniels."

He took her hand. It felt very small and warm in his. "Ryan Walker."

She smiled again, and it lit up the cold, hard

afternoon like a bonfire. His heart skipped a beat. "Nice to meet you," she said.

BEFORE HEADING to Miss Penny's for the show and tell, Ryan ran Auggie and Edgar back to the motel. They were all dead tired and cold to the bone, but the job was done. The guys were going to catch some sleep, and then they'd all hit the road when Ryan returned. It was Christmas Eve, and Edgar wanted to get back to his kids by Christmas morning. Like Ryan, Auggie didn't have family of his own, but his nieces would be disappointed if he wasn't there to watch them open their presents tomorrow.

Ryan took a hot shower and put on his cleanest clothes. He even went the extra mile and shaved. His stubble had been approaching yeti-status, and he didn't want to give the little kiddies a fright.

Auggie knocked on his door just as Ryan was lacing up his boots.

"Well, don't you look pretty," Auggie said with friendly sarcasm. Then he gave Ryan a hard look. "We're leaving in a few hours, remember. No overnighters."

Ryan held up his hands in the universal sign of innocence. "I'm just going over there to show the kids the truck, that's all."

"Yeah, right. And the fact that their foster mom is a knockout doesn't come into play at all."

"Nope. We're out of here, man." The thought pressed a cold spot into his chest, but he went on without missing a beat. "I may not have a home to go to, but I'm as eager as you guys to get out of here. I've got no time or inclination to romance a lady who has an addiction to taking care of someone else's kids." Ryan heard the words come out of his mouth and was stung by how callous they sounded. That wasn't how he felt at all.

Auggie stood quietly, with his arms folded. "That's kind of harsh."

"Yeah," Ryan agreed. "Sorry. I don't know where that came from."

Auggie nodded. "You're tired. It's been a long day."

"True enough."

Auggie moved to leave, then turned back. "That lady knows you're not there for *her*, right?"

Ryan was surprised by the question. "Yeah. I mean, I guess she does. I never said otherwise. Why?"

"Because she likes you." Auggie turned around again. "Surprised you didn't notice that, smart fella like you."

3

Thirty minutes later, as Ryan stood in front of Penelope's house, talking to her foster kids, Auggie's words came back to him. *She likes you.* The idea warmed the cold place inside him like a small fire in a cozy hearth. Ryan's eyes wandered over the house, with its scrappy winter lawn and bare-branched tree. The place wasn't big, and it sure as heck wasn't fancy, but there was comfort in every line. It would be a good place for kids to grow up, a good place to come home to.

He pushed the thought from his mind. He was leaving in a few hours. He had no time for romance and definitely no time for romance to grow into something else, whatever that something else might be.

Ryan was a little bit disappointed that the dark-haired boy didn't join them for the tour of the truck.

He had a soft spot for that lonely little kid. But the twins, whose names were Jacob and Jennifer, were enthusiastic and kept him plenty busy.

Nevertheless, when Penelope invited him in for coffee, he went willingly. The inside of the house was shabby, but snug and welcoming. The front door opened into a medium-sized living room that was lavishly decorated with paper chains and other homemade ornaments. His eyes searched automatically for a tree, but he didn't find it.

Ryan followed Penelope down a short hallway, but his steps slowed when he saw the cluster of pictures hung on the wall. The faces of children smiled out at him from every mismatched frame. He knew they must be the children that Penelope had cared for over the years. He counted a dozen different faces and thought about the positive effect she must have had on each one of those young people. Ryan spotted his dark-eyed friend in one picture, standing off to the side. Always alone, Ryan thought. He knew the feeling.

In the kitchen, Penelope gave him coffee and poured milk for the Jacob and Jennifer. They shared a plate of gingerbread cookies, which were decorated with varying degrees of skill. Of course, that didn't make them any less delicious. If anything, Ryan reflected with an inner smile, it added to the experience.

The twins scarfed down three cookies each

before Miss Penny told them they'd had enough. Then she uttered the phrase that Ryan assumed all mothers were born saying: "You'll ruin your dinner."

She sent them to wash up and gave them half an hour to watch television. They scampered off with a minimum of fuss.

"You run a tight ship, Miss Penny," Ryan said. He meant it as a compliment, and she apparently took it that way, judging by the flush that colored her cheeks. "And you really go all out for Christmas," he added.

"The kids enjoy it." She rushed to deflect the compliment onto her children. "They do most of the work. I just supervise."

Ryan hesitated, then asked, "No tree this year?"

"Not this year. Santa couldn't quite afford it." Her face took on a sad dignity, and Ryan decided to change the subject.

"Do you mind if I ask—"

"Why I'm spending my life taking care of other people's children?"

He laughed. She had so completely understood his thoughts. And coming from her, the words didn't seem so harsh. "Well, yeah."

She was quiet, then spoke frankly. "I was a foster child. It's a hard life. When I was younger, I promised myself that I would make a better life for kids like me. And I always keep my promises."

"Wow." It was the second time he'd used that

word in connection with her, and it fit. She was amazing. He smiled at her, and she smiled back.

Her brown eyes glowed, and her dark hair glinted softly in the mellow light of late afternoon.

"Thanks for coming today," she said. "We really appreciate it."

Ryan leaned back in his chair. He felt relaxed here, almost tranquil. "Well, sure. I enjoyed it. I have to say, though, that I was sorry not to see the little dark-haired boy. What's his name, anyway? He sure is a quiet one."

Penelope froze with her cup halfway to her lips. "What do you mean?"

That little boy with the dark hair and eyes. The one who was in the woods with the twins yesterday."

Her face went almost gray. "There's no dark-haired boy here. I don't have anyone with me right now, except the twins. Usually, I have four or even five children, but right now, it's just the two of them."

"Oh, well, maybe he's one of the neighbor's kids." But then Ryan remembered the face in the pictures. "Wait. Come here, I'll show you."

He led her into the hallway. Penelope was moving slowly, as if she didn't really want to go. He found the boy's picture and tapped on the glass. "That's him, right there."

"Him," Penelope said in a faint, flat voice. "He was in the woods yesterday?"

"Yeah. He seemed kind of lonely. What's his name?"

"Stephen Webber." She stared at Ryan, and an unexpected hurt covered her face, shaping it into something sad and betrayed. "I think you should leave."

"Why?" He was shocked.

"Because I don't allow liars in my home."

"You think I would just make this up? I'm not lying!"

"Oh no? Well, there's no way Stephen Webber was in those woods yesterday!"

"Why not?"

"Because Stephen Webber is dead!" She spit the words at him.

Ryan took a step backward. What was this? Some kind of weird joke, a prank? Then he stepped forward again. "That kid is not dead. I saw him yesterday in the woods, and again afterwards, playing on the lawn with the twins. Well, I mean…" He corrected himself weakly, "Not really *with* the twins. He was…" He had been sitting on the grass, watching the twins play. And earlier than that, by the tower, he had appeared pale and lonesome. Had the boy spoken with the other children, or they to him? Ryan couldn't remember, but he really didn't think so. A wave of dizziness swept over him, as if he were standing on the edge of a deep canyon, looking down into a dark abyss.

"It's time for you to leave," Penelope said. She looked hard again— hard, harsh, and infinitely sad.

"Yeah. I think you're right about that." Whatever was going on here, he didn't need to be involved. Ryan grabbed his coat and headed for the door. "Merry Christmas, and goodbye."

.

4

Back at the motel, while Edgar was double-checking the gear in the truck, Ryan told Auggie the whole story. Auggie listened in his quiet, thoughtful way and then spoke. "I didn't see him. Stephen Webber, I mean."

"You didn't?"

"Not at the job site or on the lawn." Auggie shook his head. "All I saw was the twins."

Ryan spread his hands helplessly. "So what does that mean, man?"

Auggie rubbed his face. He looked pale and tired. And, Ryan thought, a little bit frightened. "I think it means that it's time to go home."

The word "home" brought up an image of Penelope's kitchen, which was small, but warm and welcoming and smelled like gingerbread. Ryan shook his head. That wasn't his home.

But then he looked at Auggie, his good friend who had worked so hard over the past few days. He thought of Edgar, whose children were waiting for him. He wondered why he was still sitting there. "Go gas up the truck. I'll throw the last of my things into a bag, pay the hotel bill, and we're out of here."

Auggie didn't need to be told twice. He walked falteringly out the door on his false leg. His limp had become almost a lurch after two days of heavy work. Ryan started to pack. He didn't have much to do, really. When you lived out of a duffel, you tended to keep things pretty simple. He went into the bathroom to make sure he'd grabbed his shaving kit, and when he came back out, Stephen Webber was standing in the middle of the motel room.

Ryan gave a bark of surprise and dropped his kit. He left it there, on the floor, and just stared. His blood wanted to chill, and dread wanted to make its way across his heart. But as he looked at the figure in front of him, he just *couldn't* feel afraid. This wasn't a scary monster. It was just a little boy.

And the little boy spoke. "You have to help them."

"Help who?"

"Miss Penny and the twins."

Ryan was on the alert. "Are they in trouble?"

The boy shook his head, but then nodded. "They're sad."

"Kid, I don't know who you are or what you are. But there's one thing I do know. I'm not the guy to go rescuing damsels in distress and their foster children."

"Yes you are. You're the only one who can help." Stephen told him what he wanted. "Will you do it?"

Ryan thought again of Penelope's warm brown eyes and of her small house that was messy but comfortable, and had sheltered so many lonely souls. Could his soul be one of them?

He nodded slowly. "Yeah," he said. "Yeah, I'll do it."

HE MET Auggie and Edgar at the truck. "Guys, I know you want to get home to your families. But if you'll give me a couple hours, there's one more job we need to do before we leave."

It took them a couple hours, and then a couple more. First they had to find the supplies, and then they actually had to do the job. Neither of those things was easy. When it was done, all they could do was stand back and gape.

"Holy…" Ryan couldn't bring himself to finish the thought.

"Holy night," Edgar said reverently and kissed the cross he always wore around his neck.

"You got that right," Auggie agreed.

5

Penelope couldn't sleep. She sat in the shadowy kitchen, comforting herself with a mug of hot milk and honey, berating herself for being such an idiot. She had let that man in her house, allowed him near her children, and all the time he was just – what? A creep, she decided. Some kind of weird creep who had gotten a kick out of trying to play a sick joke on her. She lifted her chin. She hadn't let him get to her or her kids. Not much, anyway.

But how could he? It still felt as though it had just happened yesterday. Stephen had been playing in the woods and had come home with a runny nose, which turned into a cold that became pneumonia almost overnight. His life had slipped out of her grasp, running through her fingers like water. No matter how hard she'd tried, she couldn't hold onto him. The memory of him, so tiny and pale in that hospital bed, would come to her at the oddest moments, crashing down on her like a cold wave of grief.

Everyone on the block knew about Stephen. Ryan and his men must have heard the story and Ryan had decided to – what? Play this disgusting prank on her? She got an image of him standing next to his truck, talking softly to Jacob and Jenny, and then in her kitchen, complimenting her on the clumsy holiday decorations. Was it possible that such a kind person could do something so deliberately cruel? Stab her through the heart with his words, then just walk out the door as though it didn't matter? But she had to face the facts, not retreat into silly romantic sentimentality. He was gone, and good riddance. Tomorrow was Christmas, and the twins would be up early to open their presents.

Penny shook her head resolutely, got up from the kitchen table, and rinsed out her mug. She was going back to bed, and she would get a good night's rest. She wasn't going to let some jerk interfere with her much-needed sleep.

As she set the mug in the dish rack, the room went from dark and shadowy to bright and vivid. She gasped and whirled around, thinking that someone had tiptoed in and flipped the light switch.

But there was no one there. She looked at the ceiling. The overhead light was still off.

Slowly, she rotated back to the window over the sink, reaching out to pull back the flimsy curtain so she could peer outside. Her eyes widened and she gasped again, this time with delighted astonishment.

Shining down from the woods was a star, as bright as day and twice as beautiful. A smile exploded over her face. "Jacob! Jennifer!" she called excitedly. "Get up! You have to see this."

6

The three of them threw on their coats, pulled on boots, and ran into the woods, Penelope now heedless of her own warnings to stay away. She thought she knew what— and who— she would find, but she didn't dare hope.

They reached the clearing, and there he was. There they *all* were, all three of them: the angels who had taken a 110-foot monopine and dressed it up like a Christmas tree.

It was like nothing she had seen before. Rising into the air to four times the height of her house, the tree was lit with a star on top that must have been the size of a wagon wheel. Strings of colored lights draped downward in rough arcs, creating glowing rainbows that twinkled like magical fireflies in the cold night air. The sight was like something out of a dream.

Penelope moved forward, barely looking where she was going, taking in the beauty with amazement. And then she saw Stephen standing by the tree, bathed in the colored light of the thousands of bulbs that were strung from one branch to the next. The gleam reflected off him and traveled *through* him in a way that was impossible to describe and almost impossible to believe. If she hadn't seen it with her own eyes, she *wouldn't* have believed it. But there he was, the little boy who had slipped away from her in a hospital bed two years ago, standing there, looking at her. And smiling.

She stumbled to a stop next to the men and stood still, transfixed and overwhelmed. "Ryan," she whispered. "Do you see? Do you all see him?"

The men nodded, looking reverent. The twins put their arms around her, but they weren't scared. They were in awe. Stephen looked at each of them in turn, beaming his lovely smile. He didn't look sad or lonely anymore. He looked happy and content.

For a moment, Penelope thought he might speak. She longed to hear his voice in her ears again. But instead, she heard it in her heart. *I love you, Miss Penny,* he whispered. *You'll be okay now.*

Suddenly, she was laughing, even as tears ran down her face. "Stephen, I love you, too."

He lifted a hand, then faded away.

She wiped the tears from her face. As the light

that had been Stephen dwindled into nothingness, something else became visible.

"Presents!" the twins whooped. The miraculous nature of what they had just seen was already being forgotten as they saw the four brightly wrapped packages waiting under the tree. "Are they for us?"

Penelope looked at Ryan, who grinned. "Who else would they be for?"

Penelope nodded at the children, and off they went. She forgot to tell them to be careful. Instead, she turned to the men. "Thank you," she said earnestly. "This is the best Christmas gift anyone has ever gotten. It's beautiful. It's perfect. It's the most generous thing I've ever seen."

"No more generous than taking children into your home when you don't have to," Auggie said, and Edgar nodded his agreement. Then Auggie laid a hand on Ryan's shoulder. "We'll be in the truck. Take your time." As Auggie and Edgar walked away, Ryan had time to notice that, for once, Auggie wasn't limping.

At last, Penelope and Ryan were alone. He looked down at her. "I have no idea what happened here tonight."

She burst out laughing. "Me neither. I just know it was something beautiful, and I can never thank you enough." She looked at the truck. "You all are leaving now, aren't you?"

He nodded. "These guys have families to get

home to. I can't ask them to delay any more than they already have."

"Of course not. Do you think you'll ever be back this way again?"

He smiled at her. "How about day after tomorrow? Is that soon enough?"

"No, but I think I'll deal with it." She sobered again. "Ryan, what is this, exactly?"

"The beginning of something great, I hope." He took her hands and held them. "Merry Christmas, Miss Penny."

The End

Author's Note

For more stories, sign up for my newsletter at MishaCrews.com/newsletter

And To read my full-length Christmas novel *The Book of Forgotten Angels,* go to MishaCrews.com/free book, or click this link in your ebook.

Thank you for reading! Wishing you the happiest of holiday seasons, and a bright and joyous new year.

About the Author

Misha Crews is the bestselling author of multiple romantic novels and short stories. Readers have called her work "head and shoulders above the usual fare of contemporary romance novels," "absolutely fascinating," and "original." Born in Charlottesville, Virginia, Misha was raised near Washington, D.C., and now lives in the Shenandoah Valley, where she writes multiple genres of romance, mystery and adventure.

amazon.com/stores/author/B003ZNE5P0
facebook.com/MishaCrewsAuthor
instagram.com/mishacrews
goodreads.com/mishacrews
pinterest.com/MishaCrews

Also by Misha Crews

Sweetly Spooky

Be My Boo

Angel River Novels

(Old houses and family secrets)

Homesong

The House on the Hill

The Book of Forgotten Angels

Sweet Music

Still Waters

One Secret Summer - coming 2025!

Romantic Suspense

Her Secret Bodyguard

To Keep Her Safe

Short Fiction

At the Cafe and Other Stories

The Magic Hour

The Violet Hour

All I Want for Christmas is a Happy Halloween

Printed in Dunstable, United Kingdom